STITCHING THE CLUES TOGETHER

On the late bus home, Zach and Zoe sat with their bags between them and talked about Mateo's damaged stick.

"It makes no sense," Zoe said. "No matter how old that stick is, it couldn't just come apart sitting in the storage closet."

Zach nodded in agreement.

"If the webbing was going to tear," Zach said, "wouldn't it have happened when he was making his last save of the game?"

"So the only thing we know for sure," Zoe said, "is that it happened between the end of the game yesterday and the beginning of today's practice."

"But how?"

"Or who?" Zoe said.

ALSO BY #1 BESTSELLER MIKE LUPICA

THE ZACH & ZOE MYSTERIES
THE LACROSSE MIX-UP

Mike Lupica

illustrated by

Chris Danger

WITHDRAWN

Puffin Books

PUFFIN BOOKS
An imprint of Penguin Random House LLC, New York

Published simultaneously by Puffin Books and Philomel Books,
imprints of Penguin Random House LLC, 2019

Text copyright © 2019 by Mike Lupica
Illustrations copyright © 2019 by Chris Danger

Visit us online at penguinrandomhouse.com

LIBRARY OF CONGRESS CATALOGING-IN-PUBLICATION DATA IS AVAILABLE.

ISBN: 9781984836878

Printed in the United States of America

1 3 5 7 9 10 8 6 4 2

Design by Maria Fazio
Text set in Fournier MT Std

This book is for Prof. Paul Doherty,
who let me chase my dreams when I got to
his class at Boston College.

ONE

As soon as Zach and Zoe's teacher, Ms. Moriarty, had announced she was starting an afterschool lacrosse club, the Walker twins were the first to sign up.

"I didn't know you two liked lacrosse," Ms. Moriarty said, surprised. She'd been a star player in college and had always wanted to coach. Now was her chance to do it at Middletown Elementary.

"We've been waiting for a chance to play on a team," Zoe said.

Zach nodded. "We've even got our own sticks."

"I always knew you two loved sports," Ms. Moriarty said. "I guess I just never asked if you loved mine."

"You might not know it," Zoe said, "but our dad is a huge lacrosse fan. On weekends he takes us to games at Middletown High School. He said if he didn't play basketball when he was growing up, he would have definitely tried out for the lacrosse team as an attackman."

"We called them attackers when I played," Ms. Moriarty said. "And no, I didn't know that about your dad. Everybody around here just knows him for basketball."

Their dad, Danny Walker, was the best basketball player ever to come out of Middletown. When he was twelve, he'd taken his travel team all the way to the national championship for seventh-graders. After that, he became a star point guard in both high school and college. Despite his small size, he made it all the way to the NBA. Now he worked as a sports reporter on television, covering the kinds of great athletes he'd once been himself.

"Dad says that a lot of what he loves about basketball and soccer also applies to lacrosse," Zach said.

Like his kids, Danny Walker had played all kinds of sports growing up. Now, because of his job as a reporter, he had to know everything about all of them.

"He always wanted to play the X attackman position," Zoe mentioned.

Zach grinned at his twin sister. "I think he likes it because it sounds like one of the superheroes in X-Men," he said.

"Well, he does sort of play like a superhero when he practices with us in the backyard," Zoe said. "We've played so much out there, it feels like we're already on a team."

Ms. Moriarty smiled. "And now that we'll have a lacrosse team of our own, I'll take all the help I can get from you two."

Usually there were ten players to a side in lacrosse. But Ms. Moriarty decided that, as the third-graders were playing for the first time, it would be best to start out with eight. The elementary schools they'd be playing against all had eight players, too. And, as it turned out, exactly eight third-graders signed up for the lacrosse club at Middletown: Zach and Zoe, Lily, Kari, Mateo, Malik, Jimmy, and a new kid, Oliver. Oliver had just moved to Middletown from San Francisco, where he had played for an All-Star lacrosse team.

Zach and Zoe suggested they call their team the Middletown Warriors, and everyone agreed. It was a name with special meaning for the Walker family. Not only had the twins used it for their league basketball team, but Grandpa Richie had also played for a Warriors team when he was young.

Their first practice took place that Monday. Everyone was excited to get started, especially

Zach and Zoe. Because Zach, Zoe, and Oliver were already familiar with the game, Ms. Moriarty let them toss around a ball while she explained the basics to the others. Mateo, who'd never picked up a lacrosse stick in his life, volunteered to play goalie. After a few drills and some helpful tips from Ms. Moriarty, Mateo had shown good instincts in the space around the goal net called the crease. She agreed to let him stay at goal.

"Hey," Mateo said after practice ended for the day, "I never knew lacrosse could be so much fun!"

All eight team members looked forward to playing together during the week. Zach and Zoe were interested in using what they knew about other sports and applying it to lacrosse. Just like their dad said.

A week later, the Warriors were gearing up for their first game against Middletown West. It was only a scrimmage, but it would be the first time they'd ever played against another team. Today it was Zoe's turn to bring the equipment from the storage closet in Ms. Moriarty's classroom to the field. They all took turns. Ms. Moriarty expected everyone to be a good teammate. She said it was just as important as being a good student.

Even after only a week of practice, Zach and Zoe felt ready for a real game. By now, thanks to their dad, they knew how to handle their sticks and could carry the ball in the pocket without dropping it. Out on the field that afternoon, Zach, Zoe, and Kari were positioned up front as attackers. Behind them, Oliver and Malik took midfield. They could pretty much roam wherever they'd like. Lily and Jimmy were the defenders, ready to block the other team from scoring on Mateo in the goal.

Ms. Moriarty and the other third-grade coaches had agreed there would be no checking of any kind. Often in high school and college lacrosse, players would get aggressive with each other. Sometimes there were injuries. Ms. Moriarty said the no-checking rule was a way for the players to appreciate the beauty of the sport. They could enjoy the constant motion and strategy without worrying about getting hurt.

As they were warming up at their end of the field, Ms. Moriarty pulled Zach and Zoe aside. "You two look like you've been playing your whole lives," she said.

"It feels like we have!" Zoe said.

By the time the fourth quarter came around, the Warriors had found their groove. Zach loved the way he could start behind his team's goal and rush toward midfield. His dad had told him it was similiar to being a point guard. Now he pretended that with Zoe on his right and Kari on his left, they were on a fast break, just like in basketball. Except they were running on a grassy field instead of a court.

The score was 10–10 with a minute left in the fourth quarter. Mateo had just made a great save to keep the game tied. That's when Ms. Moriarty called a time-out for the Warriors.

On the sidelines, Zach said to Zoe, "I know it's only our first game, but it already feels like we're playing for the championship."

"Well, let's pretend it *is* for the championship," Zoe said. "The champions of today!"

"And you know what Grandpa Richie always says," Zach started.

Zoe grinned and nodded.

"If they're keeping score, you might as well score more than the other team," she finished.

For the last time in their first game, Zach carried the ball up the field. He passed it to Zoe. She passed it back. Then it went over to Kari. She passed it back. By the time they got to midfield, the three of them were flying in the direction of the goal.

Middletown West's best defender was Jack Arnold, a boy Zach knew from town basketball. Jack was fast. Probably the fastest player on his team.

He just wasn't quite as fast as either of the Walker twins.

Zach carried the ball in the pocket of his stick. As they closed in on the Middletown West goal, he faked a pass to Kari, and Jack moved up, thinking he could intercept the ball and get one more scoring chance for his team. Only Zach didn't pass it. And he didn't shoot right away, either.

Instead he cut behind Kari, and took off behind the Middletown West goal. It was a move Danny Walker used plenty of times in their backyard. He said if it wasn't against the rules to go behind the hoop in basketball, he could have made some great plays that way.

Zoe held her ground to the goalie's left, almost as if she was reading her brother's mind.

As Zach predicted, the Middletown West goalie turned his head to check behind him. In a blink, the ball was out of the pocket of Zach's stick and in his sister's. Then, quick as lightning, Zoe scored the winning goal for the Warriors as Ms. Moriarty blew her whistle, signaling the end of the game.

There was only one thing left for the Walker twins to do: their personal victory celebration. Zach and Zoe slapped a high five, spinning and jumping and bumping hips and elbows. Even most of the players from Middletown West had seen it before. They knew Zach and Zoe weren't trying to show them up.

But this time, the twins added a special "lacrosse-only" move, by tapping each other's sticks. It was like putting an exclamation point at the end of a sentence.

TWO

The following day, it was Oliver's turn to load their equipment into the old green army bag Ms. Moriarty kept in the storage closet. He brought their sticks, balls, and helmets out to the field.

Zach, Zoe, and their teammates were already outside with Ms. Moriarty. After yesterday's game, they were looking forward to practicing for their next one against Middletown North. They had gotten off to a great start and couldn't wait to find out how the rest of the season would go. It was like reading a good book and wondering how it would end.

On the way out to the field today, Zoe reminded Zach of another of Grandpa Richie's famous sayings:

"The best season in the world is the one you're playing right now."

"Lacrosse just started," Zach said, "and I already don't want it to end."

Zoe laughed. "You say that about every sport we play."

"Only because it's true with every sport we play!"

But when Oliver unpacked all the equipment from the bag, they could see he didn't seem as excited about today's practice as the rest of them. There was something wrong. As much as Zach and Zoe loved solving mysteries, there was no mystery about the disappointed look on Oliver's face.

As soon as he held up Mateo's goalie stick, everyone could see what was bothering him.

"There's a hole in the pocket," he said, poking a finger through it.

"But it was fine when the game ended yesterday," Mateo said, shaking his head sadly as he took the stick from Oliver. "If there was a hole, I wouldn't have been able to make my last save."

Oliver had his own stick. So did Zach and Zoe. Ms. Moriarty used the stick she played with in college. She stored it inside the closet with the rest of the equipment. But most of the other sticks, Ms. Moriarty said, were old and had been sitting in the closet for a long time. It had been years since there were enough third-graders interested in the sport to form a team.

"Maybe the webbing was just ready to fall apart," Ms. Moriarty said. "We've had so many practices over the last week, and our first game yesterday. Perhaps it was just a matter of time."

Zach nodded in agreement.

"The same thing happened with my baseball glove," he said. "The stitches came apart and my mom had to sew it back together."

Kari's eyebrows raised. "I don't mean to change the subject, but do you think your mom could sew up *my* glove?"

Zach smiled at his sister, then over at Kari.

"My sister and I," Zach Walker said, "think our mom could build a rocket ship from scratch if she had to."

Mateo was still holding his stick, staring through the loose hole in the netting.

"Bet we could fit a rocket ship through this thing right now," he said.

"I'd lend you my stick, Mateo," Ms. Moriarty started to say. "But I think the adult size might be too big for you."

Mateo's face fell.

"We'll get it fixed before tomorrow's practice," Ms. Moriarty said. "For now, let's just focus on today's."

Zach picked up his own stick and handed it to Mateo.

"Use mine today," he said.

"But it's smaller than the goalie's stick. How am I supposed to make saves with a stick half the size?" Mateo asked.

"Just think of it as a challenge," said Zach. "If you can catch the ball with a smaller stick, then making saves will be easy once you have your stick back."

That put a smile on Mateo's face. But then he frowned again. "If I use your stick, what will you use?"

"Don't worry about me," Zach said. "I'll just throw with my hands today."

"No way you're going to be able to *throw* a ball past me," he said.

"Well." Zach shrugged. "We'll have to find out."

Ms. Moriarty came over and gave Zach a high five. "Way to go, Zach," she said. "That's exactly what it means to be a good teammate."

It turned out to be a terrific practice. During one play, Zach tried to throw the ball past Mateo in the goal. But Mateo made the save with Zach's stick.

"Hey," Mateo said, "I think I'm getting to like your stick better than my own."

"I was afraid of that," said Zach.

"Don't worry about Zach playing without a stick, Mateo," Zoe said. "He's having fun pretending we're on the basketball court."

"Hey!" said Zach. "You can't deny that's kind of what it feels like out here."

They all laughed. Just being together, they turned what could have been a bad day into a good one. Not to mention a great practice. When they were finished, Zach and Zoe asked if they could bring their sticks home, so they could practice a little more in their backyard. Ms. Moriarty said it would be fine, as long as they remembered to bring them back tomorrow.

On the late bus home, Zach and Zoe sat with their bags between them and talked about Mateo's damaged stick.

"It makes no sense," Zoe said. "No matter how old that stick is, it couldn't just come apart sitting in the storage closet."

Zach nodded in agreement.

"If the webbing was going to tear," Zach said, "wouldn't it have happened when he was making his last save of the game?"

"So the only thing we know for sure," Zoe said, "is that it happened between the end of the game yesterday and the beginning of today's practice."

"But how?"

"Or who?" Zoe said.

"Oliver brought the equipment out," Zach said. "Maybe he accidentally pulled on it or something. It could have torn when he was putting everything into the bag."

Zoe frowned and shook her head.

"You saw how upset he was when he came out onto the field," she said. "That means he must have found it that way in the closet."

Then, suddenly, Zoe Walker wasn't frowning anymore. She was smiling. And her brother, who could usually read her mind, knew it wasn't because of Mateo's damaged lacrosse stick.

"Uh-oh," Zach said. "I know that look."

"And what look is that?" Zoe said, trying to sound innocent.

"The look that says you're thinking one thing: a mystery!"

"Only because I am," she confirmed. "We can get an old lacrosse stick fixed anytime. But how often does a new mystery come along?"

"With us?" her twin brother said. "A lot!"

THREE

Zach and Zoe invited Oliver to sit with them at lunch the next day in the cafeteria.

Even though he hadn't started the school year with them in September, they'd already become close friends. Not only had the twins found out how good Oliver was at lacrosse, but they discovered he was an even better teammate.

It was why Oliver had asked to be a mid-fielder instead of an attacker, which was the position he'd played when his family lived in

San Francisco. Oliver told Ms. Moriarty that he felt he could help their team the most at mid-field. That way, he could easily switch between offense and defense as needed. He was fast enough to come in behind Zach and Zoe and Kari when there was a scoring chance, then get back on defense to help out Mateo in the goal.

"Oliver is a great scorer," Ms. Moriarty told the Warriors. "But he thinks he'd be most useful to the team playing both offense and defense."

But when the twins brought up Mateo's damaged stick to Oliver at the lunch table, it was as if he'd chosen to play only defense.

"I didn't break it!" Oliver quickly said. "I promise on our friendship."

"Oh, no, that's not why we're asking," Zoe rushed to say.

"We've just got a mystery on our hands," said Zach. "Zoe and I were wondering if you noticed anything when you collected the equipment yesterday. Anything that might be some kind of clue."

Oliver let out a huge sigh of relief and smiled.

"It sounds like I'm part of a different kind of club now," he said. "A mystery club."

Zach and Zoe locked eyes from across the table, then smiled at Oliver.

"Exactly," Zoe said. She suggested he close his eyes, because that always helped her when she was trying to remember something.

"Picture the storage closet," she said. "What did you see when you gathered our stuff yesterday?"

The closet was in the back of the room across from Ms. Moriarty's desk in their classroom, C-12.

Oliver did what Zoe had asked, and closed his eyes. Then he began describing to Zach and Zoe what he'd seen.

"The sticks were leaning up against the wall," he said, "the pocket ends touching the floor. The masks and balls were in a bin next to them."

Oliver opened his eyes now.

"It was my first time bringing out the equipment," he said. "But as far as I could tell, everything was pretty much where it was supposed to be."

"Nothing seemed out of place?" Zoe asked.

"I don't think so," Oliver said. "The door to the closet was already open when I came back to the classroom for our stuff. I walked right in because I knew you guys were out on the field, and I couldn't wait to get out there, too."

"Wait a second," Zoe said. "You said the door to the closet was open?"

"It wasn't wide open," he said. "But, yeah. It was open enough that all I had to do was give it a little push."

Zach looked at Zoe.

"Was the door open when you brought out the equipment last week?" he asked his sister.

"Nope," she said. "How about when you brought it out the day before I did?"

Zach shook his head. "Closed," he said.

"That's because Ms. Moriarty always keeps it shut," Zoe said. "She doesn't want us looking back there daydreaming about all the fun we're going to have after school. So the rule is: door closed, minds open when we're in class."

"Do you think somebody might have been in there right before I was?" Oliver said. Then quickly he shook his head. "But if that's what happened, why would they tear a hole in a stick they knew Mateo needed to play?"

"I'm not saying anybody would do something like that on purpose," Zoe explained. "But maybe it was an accident. It's possible one of the sticks fell, and someone stepped on it and tore the webbing without realizing. It's dark in the closet, so anything could happen."

Zach scratched his head. "So now we've got two mysteries going," he said. "One about a hole in the pocket of a lacrosse stick, and another about an open door."

When Oliver and Zach looked over at Zoe, she seemed happier than if she'd just scored a goal.

"Why the smile?" Oliver asked, curious.

"The bigger the mystery," Zoe said, "the happier we're all going to be when we solve it."

"And now we've got our first clue," Zach said.

Zoe nodded. "That means we're finally on the scoreboard."

That night at dinner they told their mom, Tess Walker, about the mystery and their newest clue. Tess already knew about Mateo's stick from when Zoe told her at dinner the night before. She'd offered to sew the webbing back together, but the twins told her that Mateo's parents had already agreed to buy him his own goalie stick. He'd taken such an interest in the sport that they were signing him up for private lessons.

"Seems to me," their mom said, "that if you can find out who was in the storage closet before Oliver, you're going to be well on your way to finding out what happened to Mateo's stick."

After dinner, Zach and Zoe went upstairs to finish their homework. Then their mom watched from the porch as they rode their bikes on the sidewalk in front of their house. Every time they'd pass her, she'd wave at them and smile.

"Mom!" Zoe called out to her at one point. "You never stop smiling."

"If you had the view I have right now," Tess Walker called back, "neither would you."

Later that evening, they grabbed their sticks and tossed a ball around in the backyard.

After they'd put their sticks away and washed up for bed, Zach came into Zoe's room.

"If one of our teammates had done something to that stick, they would have said so, right?" Zach said.

"One hundred percent," Zoe replied.

"And we know practically all of the players on Middletown West from other sports," he added. "None of them would do anything to hurt our team, even if they did somehow end up in our classroom."

"Nobody in our whole town would," Zoe confirmed.

Then Zach had an idea. He told Zoe that he was going to volunteer to bring out the equipment for lacrosse practice tomorrow.

"Wait," Zoe said. "I was about to make the same suggestion!"

"So you're thinking what I'm thinking . . ."

"Isn't that the way it usually works with us?"

"Before I bag up the equipment," Zach said, "I can snoop around the closet for more clues."

Zoe grinned, and then corrected him with a wag of her finger.

"Not snoop," she said. "Investigate."

They high-fived before Zach returned to his own room, suddenly as excited about the next day at school as he was about their next game.

FOUR

When they were back in class after lunch the following afternoon, Ms. Moriarty gave them all a reading assignment. This always made room C-12 as quiet as the school library. It was fine with Zach and Zoe Walker. They loved reading as much as they loved sports. Ms. Moriarty always said that reading was just about the greatest adventure of all.

"There's still nothing better than the first page of a really good story," Ms. Moriarty often told her class. "Once you open that book, you're stepping into the writer's imagination, and your own. Then you get to take a magical journey together."

They had been reading for only a few minutes when Zach and Zoe looked up at the same time. They weren't the only ones. It seemed the entire class had lost their concentration all at once, and it didn't take long to figure out why. There was a sudden and persistent scratching sound loud enough for everyone to hear.

Neither Zach nor Zoe said anything. The rules for reading time were the same as the ones about the storage closet door:

Mouths closed and minds open.

So Zoe looked at up their teacher and tapped her ear, as if to say, *Are you hearing what the rest of us are hearing?*

"Okay," Ms. Moriarty said. "I'm going to be the one to break the no-talking rule. Because we appear to have some background noise today."

"What is it?" Malik asked, looking around.

"Probably the branches from the trees outside," Ms. Moriarty said. "Mr. Parker said he needs to hire someone to trim them back."

Mr. Parker wasn't just the custodian at Middletown Elementary. He was one of the most popular people in the whole school. Zach and Zoe noticed he was always working to make things better for all the kids in every classroom.

"It's likely just some dry branches scraping against the roof," Ms. Moriarty said. "See if you can block out the noise as best you can and get back to your reading."

Before they did, the twins glanced over at each other. Once again, it was as if they were sharing the same brain. They wondered if the scratching sound from outside their classroom might be a clue about what had happened inside just days before.

The twins prided themselves on how they could dedicate their full attention to any task, whether it was sports or a school assignment. But there were too many distractions now for them to concentrate on reading. The mystery of Mateo's lacrosse stick, the open closet door, and now a scratching noise in their classroom.

On top of everything else, a sudden rainstorm came though Middletown, which meant lacrosse practice was canceled.

Without a practice, the twins would take the regular bus home as soon as the bell rang. That meant Zach would have to wait another day to get back inside the storage closet.

On the bus ride home, Zach could tell that something was bothering his sister.

"You look worse than Mateo did when he found out his stick was broken," Zach said.

"I *feel* worse," Zoe said.

Zach nudged her shoulder. "We still have time," he said. "The closet isn't going anywhere."

"I know," she said, "but all we ended up with today is a whole lot of waiting. Waiting for you to get inside the closet. Waiting for our next practice."

"But what about the scratching noise?" Zach said. "That might have been a clue."

Now Zoe smiled.

"Aren't you always telling me that you don't get any points for what *might* have happened?" she teased.

"You mean like a basketball shot you thought was going in, but didn't?"

"Right," Zoe said.

"But remember something from all the other mysteries we've ever solved," Zach said. "Sometimes the things that don't make sense in the middle of a mystery make perfect sense after we've solved it."

"You're right," Zoe said. "And we *are* going to solve the mystery of the damaged lacrosse stick."

"We're going to stitch this whole thing together like Mom did with my baseball glove," Zach said.

He reached over with his fist, and Zoe bumped it with her own.

"It's still just the first quarter," Zach said to his twin.

Zoe nodded. "And Dad says nobody ever wins the game in the first quarter."

"Or loses it."

FIVE

At dinner, Danny and Tess Walker asked the twins if they'd made any progress solving their latest mystery.

"Well, today in class, there was a scratching noise that seemed to be coming from the roof," Zoe said. "Ms. Moriarty thought it was just the tree branches rubbing up against the building."

"We're not even sure if that's a real clue," Zach said. "But it's something."

"Except," Zoe said, "Ms. Moriarty let me run behind the school before Zach and I got on the bus. I didn't see any limbs touching the outside of our classroom."

Zach cleared his throat. "Zoe didn't tell me where she'd been until we were riding home," he said. "For a while there, I thought I might have to solve the case of my missing sister."

Zoe grinned at her brother.

"I was just investigating," she said. "Like you're going to do tomorrow when you look around the storage closet."

Now Zach was the one grinning, just at their parents.

"She thinks she's the lead detective," he said, throwing a thumb in Zoe's direction.

"Do not," Zoe said. "We're equals."

"As long as you're the equal in charge," Zach said, and everyone at the table laughed.

"I just want to figure this out so badly," Zoe said, slumping in her chair.

Zach chuckled. "That's no surprise."

"And," their dad said, placing a hand on Zoe's shoulder, "I have complete confidence that the two of you will crack this case the way you do every mystery."

They had finished their dessert by then. Strawberry shortcake, one of the twins' favorites. But none of the Walkers were in any rush to leave the table. It was everybody's favorite part of the day. The twins got to tell their parents everything that had happened at school.

But it was more than just Zach and Zoe talking. It was the way their parents listened. Tess Walker told the twins that it was a rare gift to be a truly good listener.

"I don't want either one of you to get discouraged," Danny Walker said. "Just do what you always do, in school or in sports: power through when you get to the hard parts. This is just like a game. Not everything is going to go your way."

"We didn't even get to practice today," Zoe said, resting her head in her hands. "It started raining right before the bell rang. By the time the clouds were gone and the sun came out, our bus was almost all the way home."

"Well," Tess Walker said, "if you need some sports activity, the weather outside looks pretty sweet right now."

"How about we take our minds off lacrosse for a few minutes," Danny Walker said, "and play a little Walker family basketball in the driveway."

"But, Dad," Zach said, "it's lacrosse season right now."

"Your dad knows that," Tess Walker said. "But in his heart, basketball is never out of season."

They all quickly cleared the dishes and put them in the dishwasher. Zach and Zoe were already wearing their sneakers. Their parents went to get theirs. It was decided that tonight it would be the Walker women against the Walker men.

The twins noticed their mom was wearing new sneakers.

"Do you think those shoes are going to make you faster, Mom?" Zach asked, winking in her direction.

"Totally," she said. "Even though I was always quick enough to guard your father when we were your age."

"Oh yeah," Danny Walker said. "At least in your mom's dreams."

"Uh-oh," Zoe said. "It sounds like it's game on already."

"May the best team win," Zach said.

They decided to play a game of seven baskets. The first team to reach seven won. Zach and his dad got ahead, 5–2. The last basket had come on a nifty pass from Zach. He didn't go behind the basket hanging above the garage, like he had in lacrosse. Instead, he dribbled from one corner to the other. Then he made a pass to his dad at just the right moment. Danny Walker cut for the basket and scored.

Tess Walker apologized to Zoe.

"Turns out I'm a little slow in my new, fast sneakers," she said.

But when Zoe threw her the ball in the next play, Tess Walker sunk her longest basket of the game.

"Yeah, Mom!" Zoe said, and ran in for a high five.

It was finally 6–6. Zoe and Tess had the ball. Zoe was dribbling outside when she said, "Let's get good spacing, Mom."

"My little girl sounds like a coach," Danny Walker said.

"That's because she is," Zach said. "In everything."

"Now let's see her crack the case of our stellar defense," their dad said.

Tess waved her arms to show she was open. Danny gave her lots of space, almost daring her to take the last shot. But Zoe faked a pass and drove between her dad and brother for the layup that won the game.

"Tomorrow we're back to being on the same team," Zoe said to her brother, taking a deep breath.

"Exactly where we want to be," Zach said.

"Powering through," Zoe said. "Right, Dad?"

SIX

As soon as his teammates started for the field the next afternoon, Zach went straight for the closet in room C-12. It felt like he was moving in on the goal.

Today, the door was closed, the way it always was except on the day Oliver gathered the equipment.

Zach opened the closet door and slowly and carefully looked around the space. He knew practice couldn't start until he got there. But he also wanted to search the room thoroughly so he could report any clues he found to Zoe. Everything seemed to be in order. The lacrosse sticks, including Ms. Moriarty's and Mateo's new goalie stick, were leaning against the wall. The helmets and balls were in the bin.

One thing Zach did notice was a few crumbs that looked like they might have come from a cracker or cookie. He found them on the floor near the sticks, but figured Mr. Parker hadn't had a chance to sweep up yet. They were probably left over from their afternoon snack.

Zach grabbed the green army sack on the shelf and used it to start packing up the sticks, helmets, and balls. He slung the bag over his shoulder and headed outside—though he couldn't help but feel a little disappointed that he wouldn't be bringing a good clue back to Zoe.

But as Zach walked down the hallway, he passed Mr. Parker's office and noticed the door was open. He could hear Mr. Parker talking to someone on the phone.

Zach didn't want to eavesdrop. But it wasn't as if Mr. Parker was keeping his voice low. So he slowed down just a bit. Right then, he heard Mr. Parker say, "Sounds like C-12 might be having the same issue."

He didn't say what the "issue" was, but Zach could feel his heart start to beat more rapidly. Because C-12 was their classroom.

Zach ran the rest of the way down the hall and out to the field. He ran as hard as if practice had already started. It couldn't be just a coincidence that Mr. Parker was talking about an "issue" in their classroom right as they were trying to solve one about Mateo's damaged lacrosse stick.

Zach was nearly out of breath when he got to the field. But Zoe could see the excitement on his face. She figured Zach had news for her. Maybe another clue.

"I knew it!" she said. "You found something!"

"Well, I found something out," Zach said, and told her about what he'd overheard from Mr. Parker's office.

"Did you ask what he meant?" Zoe said.

"I didn't want him to think I was sneaking around and listening to his private conversations," Zach said. "Even though I kind of was."

"So," Zoe said, "is this another mystery, or is it part of ours?"

Before either of the Walker twins could answer that question, Ms. Moriarty told them it was time to stretch for practice. She was big on stretching before any kind of sports activity. Taking the time to stretch, she said, was the best way to protect your body from muscle pulls and other injuries.

As the twins ran out to the middle of the field to join their teammates, Zach said to Zoe, "I forgot to tell you something else." Then he lowered his voice. "There were crumbs on the floor inside the closet."

"Hmm. That could be anything," she said, stretching her hamstring. "Maybe it was left over from snack time."

"That's what I thought, too," Zach agreed. Though he wasn't quite sure.

"Okay, everyone!" Ms. Moriarty called. "Come and grab your sticks."

Zach and Zoe had brought their sticks from

home, so they played catch while the others ran to the equipment bag.

Practice was only just beginning, but Zach and Zoe felt as if they'd already accomplished a lot. In one afternoon, they had two new clues, and two good ones:

Mr. Parker's call.

And the crumbs.

"You really think the crumbs have something to do with it?" Zoe asked.

"I do," said Zach. Then he smiled. "Twin clues today."

"Like us!" she said.

SEVEN

They could tell how much fun Ms. Moriarty was having teaching lacrosse, especially to third-graders who'd never played before. It was as if she was experiencing everything she loved about the sport all over again.

So today they worked more on passing, spreading the field, and making the right decisions with the ball. She made sure to give everyone a chance to shoot on the goal. The defenders and midfielders moved up, and the attackers moved back. Ms. Moriarty told them she wanted everybody to see the game from every possible angle.

"On my college team," she said, "each one of us could have played every position on the field."

"Middletown North is going to think we have more players than they do," Zach said.

"They might get dizzy trying to keep track of us," said Zoe.

"Then before they know it, the ball will be behind their goalie," Oliver said.

About ten minutes before practice was scheduled to end, Ms. Moriarty blew her whistle. "Let's finish up the day with a four-on-four scrimmage," she yelled across the field.

"But we've only got seven players," Kari said. Jimmy was out sick today.

Ms. Moriarty winked at Kari. "But when your coach gets her stick," she said, "we'll have eight."

While Ms. Moriarty walked over to the old army bag to grab her adult-sized stick, Zoe returned to her favorite subject: Mateo's damaged one.

"If Mr. Parker was talking about room C-12," Zoe said, "then it's possible he's also trying to solve a mystery inside our classroom."

"We just have to find out if it's the same as our mystery," Zach said.

"Or," Zoe said, onto something, "Mr. Parker could be *part* of our mystery. What if he's the one who left the closet door open that day?"

"Of course!" said Zach. "But what about the crumbs? Do you think they're still a clue in the mystery of Mateo's stick?"

"You know what I really think?" Zoe said. "I think we have all the pieces to the puzzle right in front of us. All we have to do is figure out how to put them together."

"They're moving pieces if you ask me," Zach said.

Then, from a few feet away, they heard Ms. Moriarty say, "I cannot believe this."

She came walking over to midfield, where all her players were gathered. In her hand, she held up the same stick she'd played with since college.

Zach's eyes grew wide. He couldn't believe what he was seeing. When he put the sticks inside the bag that afternoon, he'd missed something big. Perhaps their biggest clue yet. The same thing that had started them on this mystery in the first place.

Ms. Moriarty's stick had an enormous hole right through the pocket.

EIGHT

Zach and Zoe asked Ms. Moriarty if they could take a closer look at her stick, especially the area around the pocket.

As soon as they did, they knew they weren't dealing with scratching sounds now.

They were looking at scratch *marks*.

And in that moment, it all came together for the Walker twins. They looked at each other and knew they were reading each other's minds. Taking a few steps away from their teammates, they whispered quietly. The words spilled out of them fast, one talking, then the other, both nodding the whole time. After a minute, they started laughing. They couldn't help themselves. This last clue had pulled everything together for them, and they finally had the mystery figured out.

It was as if they could see the puzzle coming together in front of their eyes. Ms. Moriarty's stick was the final piece.

"I'll be right back," Zoe said.

She turned and ran inside the school building, down the hallway toward Ms. Moriarty's classroom. Once inside, she opened the closet and pulled out Mateo's old stick. Taking a quick glance at the hole in the netting, she smiled to herself. Then she took off again and joined her teammates outside. A little out of breath, she held out the stick to Zach, who instantly saw what she did. He nodded in agreement and grinned at Zoe.

"Both sticks have the same scratch marks," Zoe said out loud.

"Only they're not scratch marks, really," Zach said.

"You're right. They almost look like . . . bite marks," Zoe said, gripping the lacrosse stick more firmly.

"It's why we know who did it," Zach said to their teammates.

"More like *what* did it," said Zoe.

"Are you going to end the suspense for the rest of us?" Ms. Moriarty said. By now, everyone was crowded around Zach and Zoe, waiting to hear how they'd solved the mystery.

Zach was holding Mateo's stick. Zoe was holding Ms. Moriarty's.

"Zach and I think the only way this could have happened is if a small animal chewed through the netting," Zoe said. "Maybe a mouse."

"Or something with sharper teeth, like an opossum," Zach added.

He had always loved looking at pictures of opossums and small creatures in their mom's books about wildlife. Tess Walker knew the names of as many animals as Zach did baseball and basketball players. Their mom's interest in nature gave Zach and Zoe a fuller appreciation of the world around them.

"Zach knows a lot about opossums," Zoe said.

"So I know that if we find one when we get back to class, we need to be careful."

The rest of the Warriors players were listening closely as Zach continued.

"My mom showed us a video of them one time," he said. "They can get pretty frisky."

"But the two frisky Walker twins still haven't explained how they solved the mystery," Ms. Moriarty said.

"Wait," said Zoe. "You mean we get to be the teacher this time?"

"Go for it!" Ms. Moriarty said. "I think

we're all pretty anxious to find out how the hole wound up in Mateo's stick. And mine."

All the kids nodded. Ms. Moriarty sat down in the grass and the rest of the players joined her. Zach and Zoe remained standing, like it was show-and-tell.

"Okay," Zoe said. "The scratching we heard yesterday in class wasn't the wind or the trees. It had to be our little friend hunting for food or crawling around on the roof."

"I heard Mr. Parker on the phone in his office talking about an issue in room C-12," Zach said. "It all makes sense now. The issue has to be that there are little critters on the loose around Middletown Elementary."

Zoe put her hands on her hips. "Nobody was ruining these sticks," she said. "But somebody was eating them."

Ms. Moriarty got up from the grass and walked over to Zach and Zoe. She high-fived them both.

"It sounds to me," Ms. Moriarty said, "as if there's still one last piece to the puzzle before we can close out this mystery."

Zoe nodded. "It's time to find our hungry little friend."

"The one who likes to snack on crackers . . . and lacrosse sticks," Zach said.

Practice might have been over, but the story wasn't. At least not quite yet. Just like reading a good book, Zach and Zoe couldn't wait to find out what would happen in the end.

NINE

When they got back to their classroom, Mr. Parker was already there. He had a flashlight in his hand and was shining it into the equipment closet.

"Maybe you should keep the kids away from here, Ms. Moriarty," he said. "We've kind of got a situation going on right now."

Zoe couldn't contain herself.

"You're looking for some kind of small animal, aren't you, Mr. Parker?" she said.

"As a matter of fact, I am," he said. "Just don't know what kind." Then he frowned at Zoe, a curious look on his face. "But how did you know?"

As quickly as she could, as if summing up a lesson, Ms. Moriarty explained how Zach and Zoe had pieced the story together.

"Even though you didn't know it until now," Ms. Moriarty said, "you had the two finest sleuths in Middletown helping you with your 'situation.'"

"What are sleuths?" Lily asked.

Zach and Zoe eyed each other and grinned. "Detectives!" they shouted, as if using the same brain once more.

"Now we just have to find out what kind of creature we're looking for," Mr. Parker said.

"But how are we going to do it?" Zoe asked. "Leaving a snack didn't help."

"How do you two know about that?" Mr. Parker asked.

"There were some crumbs in the storage closet earlier," Zach explained. "I didn't know what they meant at first. But then I realized you were probably trying to lure the animal out with food."

Mr. Parker glanced at Ms. Moriarty, and she shrugged her shoulders. "Told you we had the finest sleuths in Middletown on the case," she said.

The twins beamed. Then Zach repeated Zoe's question. "If the cracker you left didn't help, then how are we going to get the animal to come out?"

"Please don't set a trap, Mr. Parker!" Zoe begged.

"Oh, I'd never do that, Zoe Walker," he said. "Never used one of those contraptions in my life. But I've already called Wildlife Control. They're on their way over. I told them we were going to find out what's causing all the mischief around here once and for all."

"But how?" Zach asked.

Mr. Parker cracked a smile and reached into his pocket. In his hand, he held a few more crackers.

"How about we give it one more shot?" he said. "I actually think the crackers worked. I just wasn't quick enough to catch the little rascal the first few times."

He shut off his flashlight. Then he gestured to Ms. Moriarty and her lacrosse players to back away from the doorway. He didn't want anyone scaring the creature away. He gently placed the cracker on the floor of the closet and took a few steps back, whispering to Ms. Moriarty, "If you've got a good play in lacrosse and it doesn't work the first time, what do you do?"

She smiled.

"I keep running it until it does," she replied.

Zach looked at his sister.

"She means you power through," he said.

TEN

After a few minutes, Mr. Parker tiptoed back to the doorway. He had his flashlight off, but ready if needed.

He whispered to Ms. Moriarty and the kids that he'd left the crackers near the small hole he'd spotted in the corner.

Zoe peered at Zach, a smile across her face. "We solved the mystery, even without all the clues!" she whispered excitedly.

Zach's eyebrows went up. "You're right! I never would have seen that small hole. Or thought anything could get through it."

Then Mr. Parker told everybody to be as quiet as mice.

Or opossums.

Or whatever it was they were looking for.

They heard just a slight scratching noise now, far quieter than what they'd heard that day during reading time. Mr. Parker flashed a small beam of light on the corner.

As he did, the kids gasped as they saw the nose of an opossum peek out. Then, to everyone's surprise, it squeezed its whole body through the hole. It was as if Mr. Parker and Ms. Moriarty and the kids weren't even there.

Oliver's jaw dropped. The opossum was small, but he never would have believed it could fit through a tiny hole like the one in the closet. The rest of the kids were just as shocked.

They watched as the opossum inched closer to the nearest cracker.

Then something kind of wonderful and amazing happened:

Another opossum, much smaller than the first, scurried through the same hole. It waddled toward the second cracker on the floor.

Then a third one followed, and the three of them polished off their late-afternoon snack.

"Appears to be a mama and her two babies," Mr. Parker said quietly.

It took the opossums a while to finish the crackers, being as small as they were. Even the mom. By then, two women from Wildlife Control had arrived. They showed up in the classroom carrying a small cage for the family. Quietly, they told Mr. Parker, Ms. Moriarty, and the kids that they planned to take the opossums to the Middletown Zoo.

They easily herded the mom and one of the children into the cage. But the smallest opossum made a break for it, racing across the classroom, past the women from Wildlife Control. It was too quick for even Mr. Parker or Ms. Moriarty to catch.

Just not too quick for the Walker twins.

Zach swiftly grabbed a lacrosse stick out of the equipment bag, one without any holes. He tossed it to Zoe, who was closer to the door. She laid the stick on the ground just as the baby opossum ran right into the pocket.

Zoe then lifted the stick just slightly so the opossum couldn't escape from the net. She handed it off to one of the Wildlife Control specialists, who carefully reunited the opossum with its family in the cage.

"I might not make a better save all season!" Mateo said.

"And the season's just beginning," Kari added.

Then Zach and Zoe went into their victory dance, as the rest of the Warriors cheered them on. It was a team-wide celebration. The mystery of the damaged sticks was solved and everyone was glad the opossums were rescued as a family. Now they were on their way to a new home where they'd be well taken care of.

"Best mystery yet," Zach said.

Zoe winked. "At least until the next one."

JOIN THE TEAM.
SOLVE THE CASE!

Read all the Zach & Zoe Mysteries

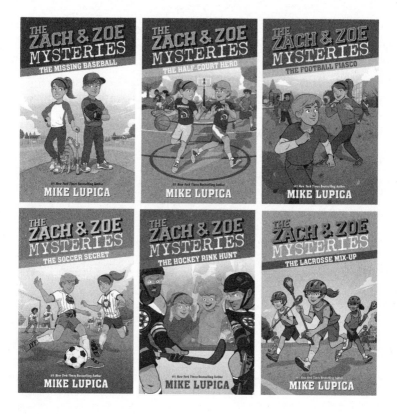